JE   Tildes, Phyllis Limbacher.
TIL   Calico's curious kittens

Calico's Curious Kittens

Phyllis Limbacher Tildes

📖 **Charlesbridge**

Pumpkin

For Beverly Anderson Twigg,
my very first friend,
and in memory of her dog, Brandy

Ginger

Published by Charlesbridge
85 Main Street
Watertown, MA 02472
(617) 926-0329
www.charlesbridge.com

Library of Congress Cataloging-in-Publication Data
Tildes, Phyllis Limbacher.
    Calico's curious kittens / Phyllis Limbacher Tildes.
        p. cm.
Summary: While Calico takes a nap, her naughty
kittens go exploring and land in trouble.
    ISBN 1-57091-511-3 (reinforced for library use)
    ISBN 1-57091-512-1 (softcover)
[1. Cats—Fiction. 2. Animals—Infancy—Fiction.]
I. Title.
PZ10.3.T447 Cal 2003
[E]—dc21   2002002258

Printed in South Korea
(hc) 10 9 8 7 6 5 4 3 2 1
(sc) 10 9 8 7 6 5 4 3 2 1

Illustrations in this book done in watercolor
on Arches Bright White 300 lb. hot press paper
Display type and text type set in Edwardian
and Sabon
Color separations by Sung In Printing, South Korea
Printed and bound by Sung In Printing, South Korea
Production supervision by Brian G. Walker
Designed by Phyllis Limbacher Tildes

Frisky

Patch

Binky

Puff

Cally

Calico's kittens are curious.
They should be napping, but . . .

Ginger is in a bag.
Pumpkin is in a drawer.
Where is Frisky?

In trouble.

Uh, oh . . .

Here comes Mama Calico!
Ginger leaps out of the bag.
Pumpkin jumps out of the drawer.

Frisky needs a bath.

What does Frisky see?
Ginger and Pumpkin
jump up to look.

Up the curtains they go.

"Come up, Puff!"

Puff doesn't dare.

Calico meows, "Naughty kittens!"

CRASH,

BOOM,

BANG!!

Down they come, curtains and all.
Where is Puff?

"Naptime!" says Calico.
"I'm not tired," says Frisky.

Frisky sneaks through the kitty door.
Binky, Patch, and Cally follow him.
Binky gets stuck, but Patch pushes
him through.

Frisky leads Binky, Patch, and Cally
across the little bridge
and across the lawn.

Cally pounces on Patch.

Binky jumps on Cally.

Frisky climbs on top.

Then one by one, they roll off.

Patch follows Cally around a tree.

Bees buzz around Binky.

What is this?

A dog!
Frisky scoots under the shed.
Patch hides under the bench.
Binky runs under the
wheelbarrow.

The dog wants to play.
He leaps over the bench.
He jumps over the
wheelbarrow.

Three curious kittens
creep too close.

The dog licks each soggy kitten.

But where is Cally?

"Meow!" Cally calls from above.
Hold on tight, Cally.

Far below, the dog barks for help.

Here comes Calico.

Binky hides behind Frisky.

Patch hides behind Binky.

Calico climbs the tree to rescue Cally.

The naughty kittens follow
Mama back inside the house.

They are finally ready for a nap.